THE GIFTS

JOURNEY

Kyrie's School Blues

By

S.P. BROWN

Illustrated by: Kai-enne Sohan

Cover art by: Jeremy Ballard

The Gifts Journey © Copyright 2022 By S.P. Brown

Published 2022

New York, NY, USA

ISBN E-book: 979-8-9852684-5-4
ISBN Paperback: 979-8-9852684-6-1
Library of Congress Control Number: 2022921960

Table of Contents

Chapter 1

The Great News!

"Guess what, Kyrie? I have a surprise for you!" Mom said.

"Am I going to like it?" I was pretty bored before Mom's announcement. Now I perked up. I love surprises!

My name is Kyrie and I am seven years old. Today started like every other day. I was sitting at the kitchen table waiting for my school work. You see, I don't go to school like most kids. My mom teaches me at home.

"I am sure you will really like this surprise," Mom responded. "You are going to school!"

"Really, Mommy? I am so excited! What school am I going to? When do I start? What will I wear?" I ran around the room, unable to contain my excitement. This was the best news in a long time. I smiled so wide that my face almost cracked!

I was happy with this great news because, even though I am seven years old, I have never been to real school. Mom has homeschooled me for as long as I can remember. That means she gives me school lessons at home. Even though my mom is not a teacher with her own classroom, she is the only teacher I've ever had. If I were in real school, I would be in the second grade.

Instead, my school building is the kitchen in our apartment. My school desk is our little kitchen table. But you don't have to think it's weird. My mom is smarter than anybody I know. She teaches me tons of words and she also taught me to read by the time I was four years old! Adults usually make a big deal about that. My favorite hobby is reading. I love reading more than anything.

My next favorite thing is making word lists. I copy down words with their definitions from the dictionary.

I also listen very closely for good words to add to my list when adults are talking. Then, I make a game of using the words in my sentences. I really enjoy shocking adults with my big words from my word lists. I call my list *Kyrie's Fantastic Words,* and I carry my notebook with my word lists everywhere I go!

My next favorite thing is singing and listening to music. I am able to spend a lot of time doing my hobbies because being homeschooled means I have plenty of time to do what I want to do. Being homeschooled also means that I don't have chances to make friends. I really want to go to school where I will be able to make friends. Now is finally my time!

I had no idea what I was in for the day I received the great news. All I knew was I was headed for a new school journey!

Chapter 2

Habari Gani!

"What's the news?"

I was sitting on the floor between my mom's thighs. She was cornrowing my hair in two braids for the week. This was my signature style. Sometimes my mom braided my two braids to the ends and put barrettes on the bottom. I always wished that my braids would hang down to my shoulders. Instead, they curl under. On special days, I would plead with Mom to leave the ends of the braids out and put them in an Afro puff. I really liked that.

"What school am I going to, Mommy? Is it in the neighborhood? Will I be able to walk there? Will you go with me in the mornings, or can I walk with other kids? How many children will be in my class?"

The questions were racing around in my head like a race car on a track. They were coming faster than I could get them out!

My mom laughed. "Calm down, Kyrie. You are going to trip over all of those questions if you don't slow down. *Usian Shule* is a few minutes away, not far from your grandma's house in St. Albans."

Oh yeah, I forgot to mention. We live in Queens, New York. St. Albans is a community in Queens.

"*Usian Shule*! That's a funny name," I giggled.

"It's different, Kyrie, not funny. *Usian Shule* is a different name because it's an independent school. *Independent* is a good word for *Kyrie's Fantastic Words List!* It means to stand alone. My cousin, Kadiri, just opened the school. If you like, we can call *Usian Shule* the US school. Using the initials might be easier for you to remember."

"The US school. I like that, Mommy. But I didn't know you had a cousin who is a teacher! That's so cool!"

7

"Cousin Kadiri was never an actual teacher, but he has been researching and creating his own plan for what he is going to teach for a long time. That's called a *curriculum*, Kyrie. That's another new word for your list!"

I made a mental note to add my new words to my list later. My mom would not like it if I tried to get up to get my word list notebook now.

"Are there going to be other kids in US school with me?" I asked.

"I'm not sure. But he and his wife, Sabra, have five children of their own, and they're all going to attend. That's enough for a classroom."

I was so happy. Even if only two other children were in my class, it would be better than my current school that was in my kitchen. The only classmates here were me, myself, and I.

"Cousin Kadiri is going to teach African customs and traditions. He also plans to teach Kiswahili! That's a language spoken in several countries in Africa. The name of the school actually means wisdom school in Kiswahili."

"I can't wait, Mommy!"

****

Everything started out great at US school. There were only a few children attending, but it felt like an army to me. It was mainly Cousin Kadiri's children, and he had a lot of them! They were:

Amani

Dalilah

Johari

Zuri

Safia

I loved their names, which all had meanings! I immediately added them to my word list! I was happy to spend time with them, especially when my mom reminded me that they were my cousins too.

There were also *Jamar* and *Jamise* who were not related to us. They were twins.

"*Habari Gani!*" Cousin Kadiri would say in the morning. That means "What's the news" or "How are you" in Kiswahili.

"*Nzuri,*" we would reply. That means fine. Cousin Kadiri taught us all of that on the very first day.

I had a lot of fun at US school. But before I could get very attached to learning Kiswahili and other interesting African culture along with my cousins and new friends, my mom gave me more surprising news.

"Kyrie, we are moving to Harlem!" I was scared and excited. This mixed into a ball of nerves in my belly!

Chapter 3

The Harlem News!

"Mommy, Harlem is so different from Queens!" I was sitting in the windowsill in our new Harlem apartment and peering out. I loved watching people.

"What's different about it, Kyrie?" She was busy unpacking boxes from our move.

"Well, there are a lot more people walking around the neighborhood, and a lot of fun sounds of cars honking, fire truck sirens, buses screeching, and people talking differently. And when we are walking outside, in some places l can hear and feel the rumble of the subway underneath our feet underground!" l said.

"Those are great observations, Kyrie."

Oh, *observation* is another word for *Kyrie's Fantastic Words List*. An *observation* is when you pay special attention and gather information about something you've seen or heard. These sounds, and the amount of people here in Harlem, are the difference between the city and the *suburb*, Kyrie. Where we lived in Queens was a *suburb*. Harlem is a city. Hey, look at that; *suburb* is another word for your list!

l pulled out my notebook. The words were coming fast today! l didn't want to miss any! l usually wrote them down the way they sounded. Then l looked them up in the dictionary later when l could check my spelling.

"l like Harlem, Mommy. But l am sad that we had to leave Queens, because now l can't go to school anymore. l had just started at US school and we left so quickly."

We had just moved and since my mom was still busy unpacking, l had not returned to homeschooling. When my dad said it was time to move, we just moved, and l really didn't understand why. All l knew was that it made me sad because I never had much of a chance to make friends. It also made me very nervous.

"Well, I wanted to surprise you, Kyrie. I have some Harlem news! Remember all those tests I gave you a few weeks ago?" I groaned. I certainly did remember. I liked to learn but I didn't love the extra work.

"Well, they were from a new school. Those tests were *assessments*. *Assessments* are the school's way of figuring out if you know all the things that you should know by age eight. You can put *assessments* on your list! You are racking up fantastic words today!"

I laughed. "I was thinking the same thing, Mommy! So, did I do OK on the tests, I mean the assessments?"

"Kyrie, you did much better than OK! You scored so well that the new school has placed you in the fourth grade, even though since you just turned eight you are supposed to be in third grade. You will start in your new fourth grade class tomorrow!"

"Mommy, Mommy, thank you! I've been dreaming every day about all the friends I will make when I go to real school! This is amazing!"

I ran from the room. "Wait! Where are you running off to, Kyrie?"

"No time to waste, Mommy! I need to go through my clothes to figure out the perfect outfit to put on for my very first day of real school."

My mom called after me. "Oh wait, sweetheart. The school you are going to is Junior Academy. It's a private school in Brooklyn. You are going to wear a uniform."

I stopped in my tracks.

"Where on earth is Brooklyn? Private school? A uniform? Where will we get a uniform by tomorrow?" I was beginning to worry. This was a lot to hear all at once.

"Don't worry, Kyrie! Your grandma ordered it for you already. Its hanging in the hall closet! And your grandma also bought you a nice wool coat with big brass buttons to match! Go check it out. A school bus will come in the morning to take you to your new school."

I was not happy about that part. We had just moved from Queens, New York to Harlem, New York City. It was fun watching all the kids outside my window walk to the neighborhood school. I wanted to meet them and walk to school with them. Taking a bus to Brooklyn sounded weird. I took the skirt with the white, navy blue, light blue, and yellow squares from the closet. My mom called it plaid. It was next to a hanger with a yellow shirt with a pretty little round collar with a navy-blue sweater vest. It was brand new. "Whoopee! All the girls are

going to have this same outfit? This is going to be cute! I can't wait until tomorrow!" When I got in bed that night, it took me a long time to go to sleep because I was so excited.

The next day, I had to get up really early to get ready. When it was time to leave, the sun was not even up, so it was still dark outside. My mom and I waited in front of our building for the bus to arrive. My mom said that it would take an hour to get from Harlem to Junior Academy in Brooklyn. I was very worried about what the bus would be like. Would it be yellow like the school buses on TV? Would it be a big bus with a lot of seats? Would there be lots of other kids to meet on the bus, or would I be all alone for the long ride? Would I make a friend on the bus?

When the bus came, it was yellow, but it was not a long yellow bus like the ones I'd seen before. It was short. I gave my mom a kiss and then stepped onto the bus. I noticed all the seats were taken, except for the two seats in the first row. Everyone seemed to be staring at me. I sat down quickly. *Is my skirt on backward?* Maybe I should have asked my mom to give me a different hairstyle from my two cornrows, which she always said was my signature style. Most of the girls seemed to have curls, ponytails, or fancier cornrow styles with beads. I pulled out my book, book 1 of *The*

Chronicles of Narnia–The Magician's Nephew, and settled in for the long ride.

Making friends might be harder than I thought.

Chapter 4

Welcome to Class!

"Who wants to tell us an important take away from the short story we've just read?" Ms. Trillinger asked the class. She looked across the room for willing volunteers.

My first observation at Junior Academy was that my classroom was so very different from my homeschool classroom. It was also very different from the classroom at US school, which had been a large room with two big round tables in it. This classroom was big enough for three long rows of desks. There were twenty-one desks in total. I counted them the first day. There were seven desks in each row. That meant it was possible for me to make twenty new friends.

I did not raise my hand, although I had many thoughts about the story. I had read the story three times. The rest of the class seemed to read much slower.

"Kyrie, we haven't heard from you today. We've been talking a lot about character traits. Can you think of any part of the story that demonstrates a character trait?"

The class all turned to stare at me. I wasn't used to this. I started to feel very warm. I felt the sweat beginning to collect underneath my shirt. This did not feel comfortable at all.

It was my third day. Things were not going horribly, but things were also not going great. I was quiet. I looked around in my mind for my words, but they were nowhere to be found. My palms felt sweaty so I shoved them under my thighs. Ms. Trillinger smiled her very nice smile at me.

Ms. Trillinger seemed really nice so far, and she was pretty. I could not stop staring at her freckles and her perfect strawberry blond ponytail. It hung down touching her neck.

Her hair reminds me of a pendulum, swinging back and forth every time she turns her head.

Pendulum was a P word from *Kyrie's Fantastic Words List*.

My classmates had not been nice so far. They mostly stared at me, and they didn't say hi.

The first and second day I smiled whenever one of the kids looked at me. When no one spoke to me or smiled back, I stopped smiling. Now, I kept my eyes straight ahead, which meant I had plenty of time to focus on Ms. Trillinger's perfectly swinging strawberry blond ponytail.

She walked to my desk and I realized that she was still waiting for me to answer. I thought for sure she'd give up. I swallowed hard and fixed my eyes on the pictures of Abraham Lincoln, Christopher Columbus, Martin Luther King Jr., and Marcus Garvey taped to the wall above the blackboard.

I tried to ignore the lump in my throat and took a deep breath. I was worried because sometimes my words got stuck. That is one of my secrets that I didn't like to share. Before I parted my lips to speak, I closed my eyes briefly. *Words, please, please, do not get stuck today.*

"The story is about hard work and sticking together. But I think that the main ch-ch-character, Joey, learned that working hard after his mom died was really difficult to do because he was so sad. He had to ignore his sadness and all the bad around him. Even though he felt all alone, he f-f-focused on his promise to his mom to look after his little brother and continue to do well. So, I know we didn't talk about this one, but I think a ch-ch-character trait he learned was *perseverance*."

The room was quiet.

Ms. Trillinger looked very surprised. "Yes, Kyrie. That is an excellent analysis of Joey's growth in the story and a character trait he displayed. Thank you, Kyrie."

The bell rang. It was time to go home. *It wasn't the worst that it could've been. My words had only gotten stuck a little.* I was so glad the spotlight on me was over.

Chapter 5

The Inquisition

Everyone was chatting and rushing out to catch their buses.

No one called to me to walk with them to the bus. If today was going to be like yesterday and the day before, no one would save a seat for me on the bus either, or ask me to sit next to them. So, I took my time gathering my things from my desk and cubby. I was the last person to leave the room.

As I walked past Ms. Trillinger's desk, she stopped me.

"Kyrie, thank you again for sharing your thoughts about the story today. Had you read the story before today in class?"

Ms. Trillinger paused but didn't give me a chance to respond before continuing.

"You've been homeschooled up until starting here. Maybe the story was one your mother came across and discussed with you?" Ms. Trillinger asked.

"No, I never read it before today, but I did read it three times today while I waited for you to start the discussion," I said.

"You read the story three times, Kyrie? Today in class?"

"Yes, ma'am. I read fast."

"I see. Well, then. Tell me, where did you come across the concept of *perseverance*? That's quite a big word for an eight-year-old. You are eight? Not nine like everyone else in the class, isn't that right?"

Ms. Trillinger's tone was strange to me. She sounded confused.

"Yes, I am eight, but I read a lot. And I really like words, so my mom taught me to copy words and definitions from the dictionary. I started with the letters S and P first to make it interesting. *Simultaneous* was my favorite S word, but *perseverance* was my favorite P word."

I was really proud of my growing word list. I kept *Kyrie's Fantastic Words List* in a notebook I hid under my pillow when I was home, so I could always find it whenever I needed to add to it.

"I apologize if this feels like an inquisition, Kyrie, but what do you do with the words after you look them up?" Ms. Trillinger asked.

I made a mental note to add *inquisition* to my list when I got on the bus. I knew what it meant from the context, but it was a great word that I had never actually used or looked up.

"Well, first I learn how to spell my favorite words, and then I practice using them when I speak."

For the second time that day, Ms. Trillinger's mouth parted in surprise. Her pause was my chance to make my exit! I didn't want her to have a chance to ask me about my words getting stuck.

"I really have to go before the bus leaves me. See you tomorrow. Bye!" I ran out of the classroom and down the empty hallway toward the main entrance of the school. Everyone had cleared out, which meant I had a bus to catch!

Chapter 6

The Unlikely Gift

I ran up the bus's steps and sat down in the empty seat in the front row.

I will get started on my homework during the long ride home. But before I could even catch my breath and reach into my backpack for my homework assignments and words list notebook, I heard a loud whisper from behind me.

"That's the new girl from our class. Did you hear her today? She thinks she's a smarty pants, but who cares because she is black, skinny, and she's ugly." The two girls giggled.

I bit back the hot tears I felt creeping into the corners of my eyes, and I started humming softly. I didn't think anyone could hear me because the chatter of the children on the bus was very loud. Everyone else was laughing or talking with friends.

I pulled out my school notebook that had my homework assignments written in it. *I will just ignore them.* I was sure I'd make friends eventually; it was still the first week of school.

My mom was in the kitchen cleaning when I came in.

"Hi sweetheart! Well, look at this long face! Did something happen in school today?"

I sighed. I hadn't decided to tell my mom what was going on at school, but I forgot to tell my face.

My face usually told my stories before I could even say one word.

"School was OK, Mommy. Ms. Trillinger seems nice enough. But none of the kids like me, and I don't know why."

My mom frowned. "Now, Kyrie, that is ridiculous. It has only been a few days, and they don't even know you. How could you even know that they dislike you already?"

"Nobody talks to me. Not even hi or bye. Nobody smiles at me, even when I smile at them first. And today on the bus, a girl from my class said I was black, skinny, and ugly. She called me smarty pants just because I answered a question in class. She sounded so mean!"

My mom was quiet for a few seconds. The expression on her face was serious.

"Kyrie, some people say mean things to others, or about others, because they are not confident about themselves. That girl is envious of something that you have, that she does not. However, mean things that other people say about you cannot hurt you unless you let them. Here is the truth: You are thin and beautiful! Your skin is brown and beautiful! And you are, indeed, a smarty pants, so she was right about one thing. She's jealous. She's afraid of your brilliance because she is struggling to realize hers. You are owning your brilliance at age eight. That is some awesomeness if you ask me! Do you understand?"

I nodded. I was trying really hard not to cry.

"Yes, Mommy. But I really, really want to make friends. How will I make friends if no one ever talks to me?"

I mean, brilliant, or not, I am really confused about that.

"Kyrie, you will find the classmates who want to be your friends as much as you want to be theirs. They are the children who believe they are smart and beautiful themselves, and they will not be afraid of your greatness. Those will be your people, Kyrie. They will appear when you least expect them. They are out there, I promise. Look at this experience as a gift." My mom smiled at the confused look on my face.

"Mommy, that makes no sense! How can mean classmates be a gift to me? They make me feel bad."

"Kyrie, there are all kinds of gifts. Sometimes they are wrapped in beautiful paper and tied with a satin bow. Your ability to read well, remember fancy words, and your pretty singing voice are obvious gifts. But sometimes, other gifts come wrapped in brown paper and are tied with string. Those gifts are our challenges. You have to dig through the ugly wrapping to find the value in those gifts. Our challenges teach us something that we need to learn. Always remember that."

"So, are the mean kids gifts because they are teaching me how **NOT** to treat other people?"

My mom laughed. "See, you **ARE** a smarty pants!" She planted a kiss on my forehead.

"Yes, exactly! They are also showing you exactly who they really are. Just think, if the girls on the bus were not openly mean, you might be tricked into thinking that they are worthy of your friendship. Then their ugliness would come out when you least expect it and hurt you even more. Now, may I have a hug?" I giggled and wrapped my arms around my mom.

I felt a little better. My mom had a way of always seeing the positive side of things.

But I didn't have much time to figure out if any of my people were at Junior Academy. I was only there for a short time. For reasons I didn't really understand, my mom decided that Junior Academy wasn't such a great fit for me after all. I overheard my mom and dad talk about how expensive the school was, and how far it was, but no one explained it to me.

My mom began teaching me at home again, but she told me she was looking for another new school. It was only a matter of time. I didn't tell my mom but moving and changing schools so much really got to me. It made me sad and nervous at the same time. My mom kept saying, "third time's a charm," which I suppose meant that next time the school would work out.

I really hoped so.

Chapter 7

The Secret

"I've enrolled you in P.S. 154. It's the local public school in the neighborhood," Mom said.

"Are you sure this is the right school this time, Mommy?" Even though this was what I wanted, I really wasn't sure if starting and stopping again would be a good thing.

"Let's think positive, Kyrie. It will be great! It's only a couple of blocks away, and you will finally be able to make friends with children from the neighborhood like you want!"

The summer was ending and the new school year would be starting. I smiled. I was glad that at least I would be starting at the same time as everyone else. Starting in the middle of the year made me the center of attention the last time, and that was not good.

"Mommy, do you think it will be strange that everyone in the fifth grade will be a whole year older than me, just like they were at Junior Academy?" I asked.

"Absolutely not, Kyrie. But if you think it's strange, no one has to know that you skipped a grade. It can be your secret that you share only with your people; the friends who earn your trust." My mom replied.

"How will I know who those friends are, Mommy?"

My mom tilted her head to the side and was quiet for a moment. "It takes time, Kyrie. In time, you will be able to identify your friends. They will be the people who really care about you, and you about them."

"How will I know if they care about me? Do I just ask them?" I asked. I imagined marching up to the mean girl from the Junior Academy bus and asking her if she cared about me. *That would definitely be weird.* I giggled at the thought.

"There are a few signs you can look for. A true friend laughs **WITH** you, but never laughs **AT** you. A true friend supports you, and you support your friends," my mom said thoughtfully.

"What else, Mommy?"

Well, more than anything, a true friend would never willingly cause you sadness. A true friend is an *advocate* for you, even when you are not there and without you asking them to be. An *advocate* is someone who has your back and speaks up for you no matter what. Does all of that make sense?"

"*Advocate*! I have to put that on my list! And Mommy, this is a lot to remember! Jeez! It seems to me that I will be keeping my secret for a long time!"

After that talk with my mom, I didn't plan on sharing my secret anytime soon. Still, knowing that I was a whole year younger than my classmates made me really proud of myself. *I was smart!* It gave me *confidence* that I would have no problem doing well in the school work that was ahead of me. *Confidence* had been on *Kyrie's Fantastic Words List* for a long time. My mom talked about confidence almost every day. It meant feeling really sure about something I am good at.

But it did not make me feel confident that I would finally make friends. So far, I had not been good at that.

Chapter 8

I Can Do This!

The night before my first day of school at P.S.154, I was nervous but I felt like something good was going to come out of this school experience. I was also happy because Mom taught me a new word, which I promptly put on my word list.

"You've been wanting to attend the neighborhood school, Kyrie. Well, here we are! Tomorrow is the day! Are you excited?" my mom asked.

"I suppose I am excited. I'm also a little scared. But I know deep down that something good is going to happen this time, so I just keep thinking about all the possibilities and that takes some of the worry away."

"That means that you are hopeful, or *optimistic*," my mom said.

"*Optimistic!* That's a great word for my list, Mommy!" I went to the bookshelf, pulled down the dictionary, and looked up *optimistic.* The definition was *hopeful and confident about the future.* Yes, that was exactly how I felt about starting at P.S. 154.

"Mommy, are you going to let me walk to school all by myself?"

"I'll walk with you the first day and we'll see how it goes."

"OK, well I am *optimistic* that you will decide that I can." My mom smiled.

P.S. 154 was very close to our apartment. It was actually on the same street we lived on, 127th Street. Our apartment was on 127th Street between Lenox and Fifth Avenue. P.S. 154 was on 127th Street between Seventh and Eighth Avenue. This meant I only had to walk two avenues west and I would be at school. I was really excited about walking by myself.

The school building was really big, much bigger than Junior Academy had been and much, much bigger than US school. The building was light blue, with white framed windows. It also had a large American flag hanging from a flagpole in the front. When I first walked up to the school, I was proud that this pretty building was going to be my school.

****

"Good morning students of P.S. 154! My name is Principal Hachett and I want to wish you all a *colossal* welcome to P.S. 154!" The public address system buzzed as the voice boomed through the classroom and hallways.

"On behalf of the entire P.S. 154 teaching staff, we are really excited about all the fun learning we are going to do this year! We will be building, building, building! And as a special building tool, every day during the morning announcements, I will sprinkle in one or more mystery vocabulary words that may appear as extra credit words on your weekly vocabulary quizzes! Pay close attention, girls and boys, there is always learning to be achieved! Have a fantastic day!"

My excitement was bubbling over! It was ten minutes into the first day of school and I already had a new word for my list! *Colossal* was definitely a new word for me!

My classroom at P.S. 154 was just as big as the one at Junior Academy, but there were a few more desks. My classroom teacher, Ms. Jones, was just as pretty as Ms. Trillinger had been, but in a different way. Ms. Jones was brown, like me! She was tall and slender and wore her hair in an Afro with a pretty head tie wrapped around the front that matched her long skirt. Her hair was black with tight curls just like mine. Ms. Jones made me feel comfortable right away. It almost felt like learning with Mommy, except I didn't have her all to myself. There were twenty-four other students in the room for her to teach.

Right after the morning announcements, Ms. Jones handed out a spelling and vocabulary assessment. All of the children had received the words in the mail several weeks before school started, so they had time during August to study. Except me, of course.

When Ms. Jones got to me, she said, "Kyrie, please don't worry about completing this, at least not for a grade. You didn't have the benefit of studying the words over the summer like everyone else. I just want you to see how my tests will be structured in the future." Ms. Jones smiled warmly at me and walked back to her desk.

I took the paper and looked it over. I knew every word and definition! My mom had taught me some of the words a long time ago! I came across some of them in my books.

I completed the answers quickly. Then I marched up to Ms. Jones's desk where she was sitting and reading a book while the students completed their work.

"Here you are, Ms. Jones. Please count this assessment toward my grade!"

As I returned to my seat, I skipped a little. I felt good! Maybe my *optimistic* feeling from the night before was because my brain already knew I could do this!

Kyrie's
Fantastic
Words

Chapter 9

The Brainiac Twins

"Settle down, boys and girls. I'm going to return your spelling and vocabulary assessments before I dismiss you for lunch. When I call your name, please come to my desk to get your graded papers," Ms. Jones said.

Ms. Jones called the students to her desk one by one. My paper had to be at the very bottom because it took a long time before she called my name. When she only had a couple of papers left in her hand, she called Dwayne Graver. He took his paper, looked at it, and scowled. As he was returning to his desk, he kicked a chair as he passed. If Ms. Jones noticed, she didn't say anything about his behavior.

Then Ms. Jones called me and Yvette James, so we got to her desk at the same time. We looked at each other and giggled. I don't think either one of us knew why we were laughing.

Ms. Jones handed a paper to each one us and said in a low voice, obviously meant only for the two of us, "Congratulations! You both scored way above average, with no incorrect questions! Please stay behind and stop by my desk on your way to lunch, both of you."

I was grinning with my whole face as I walked back to my desk. I had to pass Dwayne Graver's desk. He still wore a frown and was sneering at me. As I approached his desk he whispered, "Ugly brainiac!"

He must have overheard Ms. Jones talking to Yvette and me! I quickly looked at the floor to avoid his mean mug and any other mean words he might think of. It was a good thing I did! At the exact moment that I was passing Dwayne's desk, he stuck his leg out. If I had not looked down at the right moment, I would have tripped over his leg and fallen flat on my face! Instead,

I stepped over his outstretched leg and hurried along to my desk. *What is this kid's problem with me?*

The bell rang a few moments later signaling lunch and recess. While the class hurried out, Yvette and I hung back and waited at Ms. Jones's desk until the classroom emptied.

"*Stupendous* work, girls! Your performance on the assessment was very impressive! I can see that this is going to be a great year for you both! As a reward, you can dip into my candy bag; please feel free to take two pieces of candy. One for each excellent grade you received!"

Ms. Jones was smiling at us from ear to ear. Yvette was smiling. I was smiling too!

I was especially interested in the candy bag since my mom didn't allow me to eat candy at home. Anything in that bag would be a treat for me.

I was first to shove my hand into the candy bag and fished around until I pulled out a sour apple flavored Blow Pop! I had one once and knew it was really special, because in the middle of the sweet lollipop, there was a wad of bubble gum. I reached back in and searched until I found a Kit Kat! I loved Kit Kats! They are milk chocolate yumminess wrapped around a crispy wafer. I was also smiling because Ms. Jones had given me a new word for my word list: *stupendous!*

I waited for Yvette to get her candy.

Should I tell Ms. Jones what Dwayne said to me as I passed his desk and that he tried to trip me?

I thought about it for a moment and decided that telling Ms. Jones was not a good idea. Instead, I would do my best to ignore him. Yvette chose her candy, put it in her pocket, and smiled at me.

"You want to walk to lunch together?" she asked. I nodded and returned her smile.

When we exited the classroom door, Dwayne was leaning on the wall outside the classroom with his hands shoved into his pockets. I knew at once that he had been eavesdropping. *That is so rude!* He was frowning. I turned away.

As we headed to the cafeteria, the school librarian, Ms. Bookish, called to us as we approached the library. I recognized her because she visited our class to introduce herself and encourage the students to visit the school library.

"Girls, if you have your lunch from home, I could use some assistance stacking the bookshelves for the year. I'll let you eat while you work, and I promise you'll finish in time for lunch recess."

I looked at Yvette. We were both grinning.

"We'll get to see all the new books before anyone else," Yvette whispered.

I nodded my head in excitement. I was thinking the same exact thing!

"We'd love to help." We replied in unison.

I was so happy about my first day so far, and the brainiac twin bond forming with Yvette. She seemed really nice. I promised myself that nothing was going to remove my smile!

Chapter 10

Playground Trouble

"I need to use the bathroom, Kyrie. Meet you on the playground!" Yvette said.

We completed the book shelving task with Ms. Bookish in record time. I was looking forward to getting some reading time in at recess.

"OK, see you soon!" I said. I tied my sweater loosely around my waist and headed outside.

I sat on the edge of a swing and began reading book 2 of *The Chronicles of Narnia: The Lion, the Witch and the Wardrobe* by C.S. Lewis. I read the entire series over the summer, but I enjoyed rereading the second book. It was a really great way to escape to a land of wonderful surprises.

Dwayne Graver ran behind me and snatched my sweater from my waist. He held it out of my reach.

"Hey weirdo! New girl! What you reading—how to be a toothpick brainiac?"

I kept my head down in my book for a few seconds. I was not prepared for this direct attack. I wasn't sure how or if I should respond. Then I reached up to grab my sweater from his outstretched hand. He scowled at me and tossed it to another boy who was standing several feet away, laughing hysterically. I think his name was Corey.

"Give me my sweater back!" I said, but not quite loud enough. I ran over to Corey, but just as I reached him, he tossed the sweater back to Dwayne.

This must be some sort of mean game. I don't find it funny.

"Give me my sweater!" My voice was a little louder this time.

"Doesn't she look like a booty scratchin' African? Like the ones on the commercials when they beg for money? Yo, look at her stick legs. Listen to this: She's so icky, she so wack, she's an African booty scratch!"

I stopped chasing the sweater toss before Dwayne got to the end of his chant. I stood there looking from one boy to the other. I guess I was shocked into silence. They just laughed.

"Leave her alone! Y'all are so ignorant."

Yvette had appeared out of nowhere and managed to grab the sweater midair.

"Oh, of course, Ms. Piggy. I mean Yvette. Always minding somebody's else's business," Dwayne said.

"Whatever. You can't even spell business. Call me Ms. Piggy again and see what happens to you!" With that, the two boys ran away laughing. I figured they were off to find another target.

"Don't worry about them. They're really not very bright." Yvette handed me my sweater and sat down on the swing next to where I was sitting.

"Thanks." I wasn't really sure what to say. "You're so good at getting them to back off. How did you know what to say to them?"

Yvette stood up and put her hand on her hip. "Well, first of all I've been in school with those fools since first grade, and I'm smarter than all of them. I also know that I'm cute, so nothing they say bothers me. Plus, I threaten to have my older brothers beat them up." We both laughed at that.

Yvette picked up my book. "Oh, the Narnia series! I love these books! I've read all of them!"

"You do? Me too! I've read all seven books too, but *The Lion, the Witch and the Wardrobe* is my favorite! I've read this one about five times."

"Really, five times! That's impressive! What's your favorite part?" Yvette asked.

"My favorite part is when they go into the wardrobe and then come out in Narnia," I said.

"That's so funny. I think that there are so many other exciting parts in the story. Like when they meet Aslan. Or what about the battles? It's so interesting that your favorite part is them going through the wardrobe. That is the calmest part of the story!"

Yvette laughed. But I could tell that she wasn't laughing **AT** me, and it felt good. I laughed too. Laughing together was the best!

I thought about my mom's words about how to know when I had found "my person." Yvette had looked out for me all on her own. She stood up to Dwayne without me even asking or expecting her to. Yvette was an *advocate*! She also seemed very *confident* about herself. I decided that I could take a chance to trust that Yvette was my first true friend.

"I think it would be amazing to enter a closet in my apartment where time stops. Then, I would travel to another land and in that land, I am an important princess with powers who's not afraid of anything. Just like in the book." My voice was low.

Yvette didn't respond for a few moments.

Was she thinking about what I had said?

We sat there on the swings, rocking ever so slightly, kicking at the ragged mat beneath our feet.

"Girl, now you know that is not happening in any apartment in Harlem unless you write it yourself!" Yvette said. We collapsed into giggles. We laughed so hard that we had to hold our stomachs.

The bell rang. Lunch recess was over and our friendship was sealed. I couldn't wait to tell my mom! I really just needed to figure out what to do about Dwayne and the others who were so mean to me.

Chapter 11

The Contest!

The PA system crackled with the start of the morning announcements from Principal Hachett. "Good morning, boys and girls! I hope your weekend was amazing!"

I always got excited when I heard the crackling and buzzing of the public address system coming on in the mornings. Unlike my homeschool, there was always something new happening at P.S. 154. Usually, Principal

Hachett shared the news over the PA system during morning announcements.

I also really enjoyed guessing the fifth-grade mystery vocabulary words in Principal Hachett's morning announcements. I always paid very close attention anytime adults were speaking for any new or interesting words to add to my word list! And if the word made it onto my list, I would surely get it correct if it appeared on a vocabulary quiz.

The principal's voice continued through the crackling system.

"We are excited to announce that P.S. 154 will participate in the citywide storytelling competition for our fifth-grade classes. Participating students must memorize a storybook, speech, or fable. The challenge will be to memorize what you choose and then recite it with as much *zeal* as possible to convey the story without the use of hands or other body movements. Your classroom teachers will provide additional details for you. Good luck to all who decide to compete!"

After all the morning announcements were finished, Ms. Jones gave the extra details for the competition.

"Boys and girls, the classroom round will take place in one week, followed by a grade level round. The winners from each fifth-grade class will compete against other fifth-grade winners in a district wide competition. The winner for the district will be the district representative and will compete at the New York City competition. I encourage you all to consider this opportunity. Please put your name on the sign-up sheet if you are interested in participating."

I wasn't interested in signing up for the contest so I busied myself with adding the word *zeal* to my word list as the sign-up sheet was going around. I figured from the context that Principal Hachett had used, that it meant "energy" or "excitement." I wrote that down for now, but I would look it up during free time or when I got home from school.

As the bell rang signaling the end of the school day, I heard Ms. Jones call my name over the bell and commotion.

"Kyrie, please see me on your way out."

Oh no. What now? Did Ms. Jones see me writing in Kyrie's Fantastic Words List instead of doing school work?

I hoped I wasn't in trouble.

"Yes, Ms. Jones, you wanted to see me?" Ms. Jones was giving another student a missed homework assignment and motioned for me to wait. I tugged at my cornrows impatiently. I was really bored with my signature style.

How can I convince my mom to let me get my hair pressed to wear curls?

Ms. Jones brought me back to the present.

"Kyrie, I want to talk to you about the storytelling contest. I am surprised that you didn't sign up. Do you have questions about it?" Ms. Jones asked.

"Uh, not really. I just don't think I would be good at it." I heard the sounds from the schoolyard and glanced at the clock. Five minutes had passed. I really needed to get going.

"What makes you say that, Kyrie? You read aloud in class whenever you have a chance. You have such a nice, clear speaking voice, and you project well. I believe you have a talent for public speaking. This competition would be great for you."

I shook my head. "Thanks, Ms. Jones, but I don't think so. I have a lot of chores to do at home, and I really don't think I have the time to memorize an entire book by next week."

That should get her off my back.

"Kyrie, your reading log indicates that you read a lot at home. Is there anything else going on that you want to talk about?"

I hesitated. *Ms. Jones was really nice maybe I could trust her.*

"Sometimes, the words don't come out!" I blurted out.

There, I said it.

"What do you mean, Kyrie?"

"I stutter. It doesn't happen all of the time, and since I'm not usually nervous reading in class, it doesn't usually happen. But participating in a contest? That's different. I know that the words would probably get stuck. That's what happens sometimes. The words just get stuck."

I played with an invisible pebble underneath my sneaker. I wasn't sure about sharing this with Ms. Jones. Stuttering was one of my secrets. And I had become really good at keeping my secrets under lock and key.

"Thank you for sharing that, Kyrie. I know that is hard to share and I understand why your stuttering would make you feel uncomfortable taking on a contest like this. But I believe that you have your stuttering under control. I believe that you can do this."

I didn't know what to say. *I don't feel like I have my stuttering under control but it was really cool that Ms. Jones believes in me. She reminds me of my mom. My mom always believes that I can do things that I don't believe I can do.*

"Ms. Jones, I am not *confident* about this, but you seem *optimistic* that I can do this. I'm just not sure."

I hope she noticed that I used two words from Kyrie's Fantastic Words List!

Ms. Jones smiled.

"I get it, Kyrie. It's scary. It's something new that is out of your comfort zone. I really do understand. How about this; would you consider preparing for the classroom round next week? All you have to do is prepare to recite your chosen piece in front of your classmates. I know you can do that because you do it every day. If you decide when the day comes that you don't want to go through with it, you can withdraw without further discussion from me. How does that sound?"

I took a deep breath. It did sound like a fun thing to challenge myself with.

"Have I been *compelling*, Kyrie?" She smiled again. Ms. Jones had seen *compelling* on my list because she had asked to see it the day before when I had it out on my desk.

"Yes, Ms. Jones. You have been extremely *compelling*."

I returned her smile, took the sheet, and wrote my name on it.

Now, to figure out what to memorize. This was not going to be easy!

Chapter 12

My Voice!

It was hard for me to choose something to recite for the storytelling competition. There were many stories that I loved so much. Finally, I chose a folktale. The title was *Anansi the Spider: A Tale from the Ashanti* by Gerald McDermott. I saw it for the first time at US school. I used to read the story aloud all the time when I was there.

I memorized the story on the weekend before the competition. Memorizing was easier for me than I imagined it would be. I just read it over and over until I knew it. The day of the classroom round arrived and I felt ready. I could recite the folktale without even glancing at the pages!

On the day of competition, I was nervous, but I knew I was prepared to do a good job. There were three other classmates, plus me, competing. Ms. Jones asked us to draw numbers in the morning to decide the order we would be reciting. I picked the lowest number, so I would go last.

Dawn James was up first.

Dawn recited a passage from *Charlotte's Web* by E.B. White. Dawn wore a red jumper dress and a brand-new pair of white Nikes. I figured she would do well because she looked really nice. But Dawn forgot the story after the fifth line.

"Thank you, Dawn. You may take your seat," Ms. Jones said politely.

Dashawn Williams was next. Dashawn didn't look like he had on any new clothes. That made me feel better, because I did not have anything new to wear.

Dashawn recited a passage from *Tales of a Fourth Grade Nothing* by Judy Blume. Dashawn had memorized the passage but recited it boringly. He never changed his voice. The class clapped politely. I knew Dashawn had not been good enough.

Sherice Mathers was next. Sherice had pretty long braids with colorful beads. Sherice recited a poem by Langston Hughes called "Mother to Son." Her voice was strong and very pretty. It almost sounded like she was singing the poem. Sherice did a great job and the class clapped loudly for her.

Then it was my turn. I didn't feel confident anymore. Ms. Jones called my name twice before I was able to force my legs to stand me up and carry me to the front of the room.

I wore my favorite blue jeans with flowers stitched on the pockets.

"I love your pretty jeans with the beautiful *embroidery*!" Ms. Jones said to me that morning when I entered class. I immediately pulled out my word list and added *embroidery*. Up until then, I called it colored stitches. I also wore my white peasant top, which I loved.

My hair was in my two cornrows but my mom had agreed to give me a nice Afro puff in the back. I looked cute. My hairdo and my outfit helped me feel confident.

I reached the front of the room and turned around. I felt like there were 100 sets of eyes on me, but I knew it was the same twenty-four classmates who were always there. I took a deep breath.

"I can do this. My words will not get stuck."

Then, I found a spot above Ms. Jones's head on the wall, stared at it, and began sharing the tale of Anansi and his seven sons. The more I got out, the stronger I felt, and the less I worried about my words getting stuck. Actually, my words did not get stuck at all that day.

My voice was pretty. I **KNEW** it.

My voice was strong. I **KNEW** it.

My voice was like a melody. I **KNEW** it.

My classmates erupted in thunderous applause when I was done.

No one in my class had done it better than me. I also knew that.

I won!

After winning the classroom round, I also defeated the other fifth graders from the other classes at P.S. 154 in the school-wide competition. I went on to win at the district round and became the district representative to compete at the city competition. I lost there.

Ms. Jones told me later that no one had even come close to my performance until the city round. Everyone cheered for me after I finished speaking. After each competition, my confidence grew. People wanted to hear what I had to say. My voice was important!

I decided that it was time to do something about the kids at school who were mean to me. But I needed a plan!

Chapter 13

The Master Plan!

"What's wrong, Kyrie? Don't you feel great about winning? You were amazing!" Yvette knew something was wrong. We were sitting on our favorite playground swing during recess. I was extra quiet.

"I **DO** feel really good about the competition." A few weeks had passed since I won the classroom round, the school round, and the district round of the storytelling competition.

Although I lost at the city competition, the whole experience was a lot of fun. The girl who won was really pretty, with long hair. But she was also very good, so it was fine that she beat me. I received an honorable mention. I didn't really know what it meant but my mom, Ms. Jones, **AND** Principal Hachett said that was really good. Losing the citywide competition was not what had me down.

"I'm sorry, Yvette. I keep thinking about how doing so well in the competition made all the teachers and Principal Hachett notice me, but it wasn't enough to get the other kids in our class to like me."

"Well, did you participate to get the others to like you? Why do you care what they think about you?" Yvette asked.

"No, I didn't. I actually did it because Ms. Jones *compelled* me to. After the classroom round, I realized it was fun."

"Nice, Kyrie. I saw how you slipped that word in." Yvette gave me a high five.

I grinned at her and continued. "I wish I could be more like you. You're tough and don't let people make you feel bad. Dwayne and his friends still call me names when you're not around. The other girls in the class whisper and are rude to me. I haven't said anything to anyone because I don't want to complain. I need to handle it myself."

"I'm sorry, Kyrie. I didn't know. Has there been anything else going on?" Yvette asked softly.

"Well, Dwayne and his buddies follow me after school almost every day. They call me ugly and yell other mean things. Sometimes they throw tiny pebbles at me, but they don't ever really hit me. I've been ignoring them. Eventually they stop and go in the opposite direction, but it's horrible until they do. I thought that ignoring them was the best thing to do, but they start up again the next day. They just won't stop."

My voice cracked. I could feel the tears creeping in, but I didn't want to cry.

I will not cry!

Yvette's eyes were flashing now and her fists were balled up at her sides. She was angry.

"Kyrie, you have to do something. This can't go on any longer! We need to think of a master plan."

Yvette's anger was contagious. I could feel my courage building.

"What are you thinking?" I asked her.

"I know! Let's make a list of your options. Do you have your word list notebook with you?"

"Of course, I do! You know I carry it everywhere!" I pulled the notebook from my back pocket. I never knew when I was going to come upon a new word!

Yvette took the notebook out of my hands and started pacing, stopping only when she needed to write something down. Yvette always paced when she was deep in thought.

I sat on the ground with my chin resting in my hands. This was my thinking pose.

"The way I see it, these are your only options." Yvette handed back the notebook and I read the list she had written out loud:

Kyrie's Stop the Bullying Master Plan Options
1. Tell Ms. Jones.
2. Tell your mom (same as telling Ms. Jones).
3. Fight Dwayne after school & win.
4. Use your words to stand up to them.

"You know, Yvette, I think about option number 1 and number 2 all the time. But I talk myself out of it. If you know what I know, snitches get stitches!" We said it in unison and then cracked up laughing.

"Anyway, the words only really hurt my feelings. If anyone ever touched me, I would risk the stitches because I would tell Ms. Jones immediately!"

Yvette nodded furiously and gave me a high five to show her agreement. "Period!" she said.

"OK, so, option number 3, fight Dwayne? Nope. Not for me. For one thing, fighting doesn't solve anything except for getting into more trouble. Plus, you're right, I'd have to win for it to make a difference, and what are the chances of that?" I said.

Yvette stopped pacing and took a good look at me. "I guess you have a point. You're a bit on the lightweight side. Me, on the other hand, I'm a heavyweight. I would squash him!" We collapsed into giggles again. I knew she was only joking.

Yvette told me when we first met that she had never had a fight in her life, and she didn't plan on it. "I have no interest in risking harm to this gorgeous face!" she said.

This talk was cheering me up. It felt so much better to have a friend to help think through a problem. Plus, it helped that Yvette was funny!

When we calmed down from the giggling, I stared hard at option number 4. Could I really use my words to stand up to Dwayne's bullying? Me?

Yvette put her hands on both of my shoulders.

"Kyrie, seriously, think about it. You just won three competitions where you wowed everyone with words. You used **WORDS** to show your power! That's it! That's your super power! Your voice! Your **WORDS**!" By now, Yvette was shouting.

My friend and I started jumping up and down. We were screaming and laughing hysterically. We had a master plan!

Now all I had to do was figure out what **WORDS** I would use to put the master plan into action!

Chapter 14

My WORDS!

My SUPER POWER!

It didn't take long to put our master plan to the test.

I was walking home after school the day after Yvette and I created the master plan. I thought I had escaped Dwayne and his squad, but no such luck. I was half way home—one whole avenue away from the school, and one whole avenue from my apartment. If Dwayne decided to bully me, no one from school or home was close enough to help me.

"Toothpick, where are you going so fast? Wait up, toothy toothpick! With your buck teeth and your twigs for legs, how do you hold yourself up?"

I began to doubt going through with my master plan today. I kept walking. I ignored them as I had been every day.

"Hey, ugmo toothpick! You think you're so smart getting the highest grades and winning that dumb storytelling contest. Well, I guess you're not so smart after all, because you finally lost, dummy!"

That stopped me in my tracks. I had dealt with the mean, ugly, toothpick, and blacky remarks for weeks, but Dwayne Graver was now calling ME dumb? After I had outscored him on every single math, vocabulary, or reading comprehension assessment since the school year started.

No way! Enough was enough!

I turned around and started walking quickly toward Dwayne and the others. I guess they were not paying attention to me when I turned around and walked toward them, because they seemed very surprised to find me in front of Dwayne and staring him in the face. Before they could regroup, I started talking in a strong, loud voice. The words just came to me!

"Dwayne, why would you waste such a *colossal* amount of your time following someone you believe is ugly **AND** dumb? That makes no sense! I used to believe that you were just mean, now I realize that you are mean **AND** immature."

Dwayne's mouth was wide open in surprise. His two friends also looked confused.

I turned to his friends. One was Corey, who seemed to be his main sidekick. I didn't know the other boy.

"And **YOU** boys, **YOU** clearly don't have *independent* thoughts. You need to grow up and find some brains of your own!"

I turned back to Dwayne.

"I'll tell you what's dumb, Dwayne. Your bullying is dumb! It's not even original! I'm tired of it. I was going to let you suffer, but I decided today not to stoop to your meany level!"

Dwayne finally found his voice.

"What is that supposed to mean? You can't do anything to me, brainiac stick girl!"

I kept talking.

"I'll tell you what it means. My mom's friend lives right there in that building above us. She sits in her window every day around this time. She's been watching you and your squad scream your nasty words at me every day. She called my mom last night and told her what she saw."

Dwayne looked sick to his stomach.

"Dwayne, we both know that P.S. 154 has a zero-tolerance policy for bullying. So, my mom was actually on her way in to school today to tell Principal Hachett exactly what you all have been doing to me. Now, I'm *optimistic* that you know what that would mean for you.

"I will be expelled! My mom will kill me," Dwayne exclaimed.

"I **KNEW** you were smarter than you have been demonstrating with your bullying! It's a good thing I'm nice enough to give you a second chance. Since I wouldn't want that—even for you—I can be an *advocate* for you."

"An *advocate?* Wh-what does that mean?" Dwayne stammered.

"It means that I convinced my mom to wait until I talk to her tonight. I will agree to tell my mom that you apologized today about even appearing to be bullying me **AND** you promised to never, ever, treat me, or anyone else, mean again, even when you're just joking. But right this second, that's not true, is it Dwayne? I haven't heard you apologize yet. And I will not tell fake stories to protect a bully."

I crossed my arms over my chest to signal that I was almost done talking. I began tapping my foot to show my impatience, like I'd seen in cartoons.

"I'm waiting, Dwayne. And I'm *confident* that you can figure out how to make this right."

That did it! The words I was waiting for came rushing from Dwayne's mouth like a waterfall!

"I'm really, really sorry, Kyrie! I was only playing all this time! I didn't mean those horrible things I said. I mean, you are skinny but there is nothing wrong with that and you're really smart! And I don't really think you're ugly. Seriously! And I double pinky swear promise not to be mean to you or anyone else again."

Dwayne stopped and took a deep breath. Then he added "Please, Kyrie. I can't get expelled, or even suspended. My mom will really kill me! I'm sorry."

He looked over at Corey and the other boy.

His friends started mumbling their apologies. When they seemed to be out of words, I spoke again.

"That was a *stupendous* apology, delivered with such *zeal*. Well done! I accept your apologies. I'm certain we won't need to have this conversation again. Good night, boys."

I smiled, turned on my heel, and left them standing there.

I did it! **AND** I used seven words from my list in one conversation! That was a personal record!

That is how I found the first gifts in my journey.

Kyrie's Gifts

1. A person's meanness can teach me how **NOT** to be **AND** teach me character traits to watch out for.
2. My first best friend, Yvette, showed me what trust and caring in friendship looks like.
3. My words are a powerful gift!

KYRIE'S FANTASTIC WORDS LIST

Advocate—a person who publicly supports a person or cause

Assessment—evaluation or test of ability

Colossal—extremely large

Compelling—persuasive, convincing

Confident—self-assured or positive

Curriculum—the subjects making up the course of study

Embroidery—to sew a picture or design onto cloth using different colors of threads or yarn.

Independent—free from outside control, not dependent on another's authority

Inquisition—prolonged intense questioning

Observation—watching something carefully in order to gain information

Optimistic—hopeful & confident about the future

KYRIE'S FANTASTIC WORDS LIST

Pendulum—a weight hung so it can swing

Perseverance—persistence or determination in doing something even when difficult

Simultaneous—done at the same time

Stupendous—amazing; extremely impressive

Suburb—the outlying (or outside) part of a city, especially a residential one

Zeal—great energy or enthusiasm

KYRIE'S FAVORITE NAMES

Amani: peace

Dalila: gentle/delicate

Jamar: handsome; all wise

Jamise: may protect

Johari: jewel

Safia: friend or pure

Zuri: beautiful

About the Illustrator

Kai-enne Sohan is from the south shore of Long Island, New York, and began drawing at the early age of 10. A self-taught talent, drawing and acting have competed for equal space in her heart and schedule since middle school and through high school, as Kai-enne endeavored to fill her extracurricular time with theater activities and art clubs. Kai-enne is currently a first-year student and performing arts major at Nassau Community College, Long Island, and ultimately aspires to pursue an acting career spanning Broadway, film, and television. In addition to drawing and acting in theater productions, Kai-enne also enjoys singing, spending time with her chihuahua (Snickers), going to the beach at night, and listening to music. *Kyrie's School Blues* is the first book Kai-enne has illustrated.

IG@sohkaii
IG@kaiesoh

About the Cover Artist

Jeremy Ballard hails from Morristown, New Jersey, and has been creating visual art for as long as he can remember and professionally for over a decade. While pursuing his Bachelor of Fine Arts at William Paterson University, Jeremy began challenging and expanding his creative palette, exploring the many mediums of color, line, shape, form, and texture. Ultimately, Jeremy began honing his inherent skill set as a realistic artist, arriving at a penchant for designs achieved using a combination of acrylic, ink, and colored pencils. In addition to his various pursuits as a fine artist, Jeremy is a museum professional and enjoys a deep love and passion for the arts. *Kyrie's School Blues* is Jeremy's first literary cover art piece.

IG@jeralamar63

Acknowledgements

All my gratitude and honor to Almighty God for the abundance of blessings in my life. I am finding gifts buried within my past and present experiences every day. I'm humbled to have heard the call to impact lives through writing stories and the gifts inform my stories, so I am extremely thankful.

I thank God for both the visionary and logistical angels deposited in my life to spotlight and guide my path. You know who you are. Special shout out of gratitude to Ayanna Mills, my literary coach, who brought this first installment of The Gifts Journey Series to fruition, merely based on my ask.

And an endless standing ovation to the really special people; the educators who selflessly devote their lives to the ongoing enrichment and development of children. You hold one of the most vital roles society produces. Thank you for all you do.

S.P. Brown

About the Author

S.P. Brown is an attorney, corporate executive, education consultant, youth development leader, author, and speaker. *Kyrie's School Blues* is book one of The Gifts Journey Chapter Book Series and is S.P. Brown's first children's book. S.P. discovered her love of reading and words as a young child and began creative writing in her childhood, initially through songwriting. As an adult, S.P. has been writing creatively as a hobby for the last fifteen years.

S.P. 's personal passions are her faith in God, youth and women empowerment, promoting positive mental health awareness for herself and others and advocating in the interest of eradicating domestic violence and all forms of interpersonal violence.

S.P. received her bachelor of arts, magna cum laude, from Hunter College, City University of New York, in human communications and her Juris Doctor from St. John's University School of Law. She lives in the New York area and is a health and fitness enthusiast. In addition to writing, in her free time she enjoys singing, weight lifting, Peleton riding, meditation and prayer.

S.P. Brown is also the author of *Gifts in Brown Paper Packages*, her first novel published in 2021.

Follow S.P. Brown: IG @s.p.brownwrites
Facebook @spbrownwrites.

And on the web @ http://www.spbrownwrites.com

Made in USA - Kendallville, IN
94708_9798985268461
12.21.2022 1413